THE TORTOISE
AND THE BIRDS

retold by Jay Dale

illustrated by Alessia Trunfio

a Capstone company — publishers for children

Engage Literacy is published in the UK by Raintree.
Raintree is an imprint of Capstone Global Library Limited, a company incorporated in England and Wales having its registered office at 264 Banbury Road, Oxford, OX2 7DY – Registered company number: 6695582

www.raintree.co.uk

Editorial credits
Erika L. Shores, editor; Charmaine Whitman, designer; Katy LaVigne, production specialist

10 9 8 7 6 5 4 3 2 1
Printed and bound in China.

The Tortoise and the Birds

ISBN: 978 1 4747 3915 3

Contents

Chapter 1
FOOD TO SHARE

A long time ago when earth was new,
odd people lived above the clouds.
The animals on earth knew
about these "cloud people",
but only the birds had ever met them.
These cloud people were good and kind.

For many years earth was brown
and dry from lack of rain.
Plants did not grow and the animals
were hungry.
So the cloud people said they would help.

"All the animals with wings can come
to our home," the cloud people said.
"They can fly up to us,
and we will feed them.
We have plenty of good food to share."

The birds were very happy about this news.
They all met on a large rock
to talk about the visit.
Two tortoises lived in a hole under the rock.
The wife was away looking for food,
but her husband was at home.
He listened to the birds as they talked.
As the birds chatted about all the food
they were going to eat, the tortoise
stuck out his head.
"Please take me with you," he said.
"I am so, so hungry."

The birds felt sorry for the tortoise.
They each gave him a colourful feather.
Then they tied the feathers to his feet
so he could fly.
The birds laughed at the tortoise
because he looked so funny.
"What will we call this tortoise
if the cloud people should ask his name?"
asked a bright green parrot.

"Let's call him 'All of You',"
said another bird.
"Because he looks like all of us."

"He can be our king," the parrot laughed.
"We will call him King All of You."

Chapter 2
GREEDY TORTOISE

The birds and the tortoise got ready to fly.
Then they went up, up, up into the sky
until they finally reached the cloud people.

The cloud people were very happy to see them.
They had cooked large amounts of food
for everyone.
"Who is this food for?" asked the birds.
"It is for **all of you**!"
answered the cloud people kindly.
"We made it for all of you."

The greedy tortoise knew his new name.
So he quickly grabbed the food
and ate nearly all of it!
He left only a few crumbs for the birds.
The cloud people were very surprised.
They thought this must be
what kings from earth did.

Chapter 3
CRACKED SHELL

The birds were upset with the tortoise
for eating nearly all of the food.
So they took all their colourful feathers back.
Then they said goodbye to the cloud people,
and went straight back down to earth
without the tortoise.
Only the parrot was left.

"Will you help me, dear parrot?"
the tortoise asked.
"When you go back to earth,
please tell my wife to put out
some soft grass and leaves for me.
Then when I fall back to earth,
I will land on something soft."

The parrot did tell the wife,
but he got the story mixed up.
He told her to put out rocks
for the tortoise so he had something
to land on.
So when the tortoise fell down to earth,
his shell was cracked into large
and small bits.

The tortoise's wife took care of him
day and night.
She tried to put his shell back together
as it had been, but it was never
the same again.